This book belongs to:

_____

Aaron's Gratitude Rock

Sukaina Amirali Mukhtar

Table of contents

Relaxation and Meditation   5
Mindful Message for Adults   7
Message on Gratitude   8
Story: Aaron's Gratitude Rock   9
Thinking Time   30
What can we learn from the story?   31
Magical phrases   32
Gratitude tree   33
Colouring words of affirmations   34
Colouring Positive Pete and Mindful Molly   36
Famous quotes   37
Journaling   40
Quotes by Positive Pete and Mindful Molly   41
Glossary   45

Relaxation and Meditation

Relaxation and meditation have a range of benefits; visualisation, creativity and focus are just a few of many that can leave an imprint. It is important to understand that we all need space and time to reflect.

Close your eyes and take a deep breath in through your nose for 5 seconds and breathe out for 5 seconds. You must breathe slowly. Form a circle with your lips when you breathe out. Repeat this 5 times.

Imagine yourself strolling in a lush, green forest with colourful birds chirping around you. The long grass brushes gently across your bare feet. You feel a cool breeze blow around you, whispering messages in your ears, which you repeat to yourself.

I can make myself happy

I am smart

I am grateful

I can do it

You look above and see a graceful, white dove sitting on a bent branch. It calls out to you to stroke and hold it. You move your hand slowly to brush its wings and bring it close to your chest, showing it warmth and love. As it perches upon your hands, it looks towards the sky and flies off.

You take a deep breath in and out, filling yourself with the peace and silence around you. Keep your eyes closed for some time and continue to take deep breaths, clearing your mind of any thoughts.

Mindful Message for Adults

Critical thinking, reflection, mindfulness, gratitude and resilience are a few of the many tools that children should be taught in order to prepare them for the life ahead of them. Emotional intelligence is crucial for the wellbeing of a child. Providing these tools at a young age will inspire them to have hope and work through their challenges as they get older.

As parents and teachers, we cannot continue to hold their hands but must provide them with the means required to excel and become individuals who work together in this global village.

Having a role model or reading stories from the lives of others enables the child to learn and accept the truth, that there is light at the end of the tunnel. There is hope when you feel discouraged. You just need to find the strength within you.

People who have been successful or have had a profound influence and a positive impact on society also have flaws. Success is not a result of perfection, but of tapping into your potential and working consistently hard at something that you are passionate about. Teaching children these skills will enable them to reach for their stars, despite rain or storm.

Message on Gratitude

A deep sense of gratification and the actualisation of what we are blessed with, enables us to feel a sense of contentment. Contentment which results in empowering our thoughts from spiralling downwards towards negativity. Gratitude is a powerful concept which resonates in many hearts if introspection is the path taken.

If we enable children to make gratitude a habit, they will acquire a great tool to strengthen their mindset. It will help them deal with discontent that may result from daily and inevitable comparisons with their friends, or it may reduce their demands for instant gratification if they are taught the skills to be content with what they have in the present. This will result in cultivating patience, resilience and happiness.

Positive Pete and Mindful Molly

Aaron's Gratitude Rock

You are your own super hero!

It was early one morning when Aaron woke up and picked up his 'gratitude rock.' Every morning he held his special rock to remind him to be grateful for what he had. He started his day positively by picturing how he wanted his day to be and everything that he had to look forward to. He thought of the smell of fresh air and the different trees that surrounded him, the warmth of the sun and the cool breeze, were only a few of many fond images he created. He pictured himself smiling and greeting people. He knew that by smiling, he would often make others smile. Everyday was his chance to make a difference.

It was the summer holidays and Aaron was preparing for a school entrance exam. He had spent many days during that summer practising, but he always felt that learning was for life, not just for his exam.

His older sister, Danisa, was preparing for the cricket trials to make it into her dream team, which were going to take place at the end of summer. She was passionate about playing cricket, and wanted to play for England in the near future. Sometimes her fear of failure held her back from performing well. Positive Pete would remind her to overcome her fears by believing in herself, to accept and learn from her mistakes, and not to give up on what she was passionate about.

As the summer was coming to an end, the days for the entrance exam and the trials were nearing. Aaron could feel himself becoming anxious, so he started to meditate and visualise in order to attain inner peace and positivity, as advised by Mindful Molly. He closed his eyes and took deep breaths in and out to relax himself. He pictured himself looking at the paper, with a big smile on his face.

Danisa found it difficult to understand the importance of meditation. She also felt anxious but acted like it did not bother her.

It was the 3rd of September , the day of Aaron's exam. He sat with the paper in front of him and closed his eyes for a moment, visualising himself receiving the marked exam paper with an excellent grade. He opened his eyes, picked up the pencil and started to write.

Mindful Molly: Well done for visualising positive thoughts!

On the same day, Danisa had her trials to make it into the cricket team. Firmly holding the bat, she saw the ball coming at a fast pace and was surprised at the speed of the ball. Her fear took over and she lost her confidence. The ball hit the wicket and she was out. Given a few more chances, she continued to try but was unable to get the bat on the ball, and lost hope. As she left the trials, she could not hold back her tears.

Positive Pete: Don't worry Danisa, you will get another chance. Don't hold back your tears. Everyone has their challenges and will feel sad sometimes. Many successful people have not achieved their goal after their first attempt. Making mistakes, or not succeeding, is all part of learning.

Danisa sat in her bed that night, thinking about her day but trying to be more positive.

Mindful Molly: Danisa, you tried your best and put in the effort. Do not lose hope. Learn from your weakness and strengthen yourself. You can always try again. Overcome your fear and do not doubt yourself.

Positive Pete: Be confident with who you are and remember, making yourself happy is in your hands. Everyone gets nervous. Everyone makes mistakes. Persevere. Be positive.

Mindful Molly: Ask for what you want. Believe in it. You may doubt yourself and feel sad but make yourself feel as if you have already accomplished it, and remember how good that thought makes you feel. Your feelings are very important.

Danisa took out her journal to write down her thoughts and feelings. She drew pictures and wrote a poem to express her emotions. After some time, she closed her eyes and fell asleep; dreaming of what her future could be.

Aaron lay awake in his bed reading his book. He was grateful for the opportunity to sit the exam and to gain knowledge in the process. No longer worrying about how he performed, he cleared his mind then meditated before he slept.

Mindful Molly: Do not think about the past or worry about the future. Allow yourself to appreciate where you are in the present.

Thinking Time

1. How do you think meditation helped Aaron?
2. What can Danisa do differently and how do you think
 this will help her?
3. How do you think fear stops you from succeeding?
4. Why do you think Danisa cried?
5. Was it okay for her to cry? Why or why not?
6. What is your passion or what is really important to you
that you love to do? What can you do to achieve it?
7. Have you ever been afraid of doing something? Why?
What did you do to overcome your fear?

What can we learn from the story?

When you are going through a challenge, remember there is so much to be grateful for.

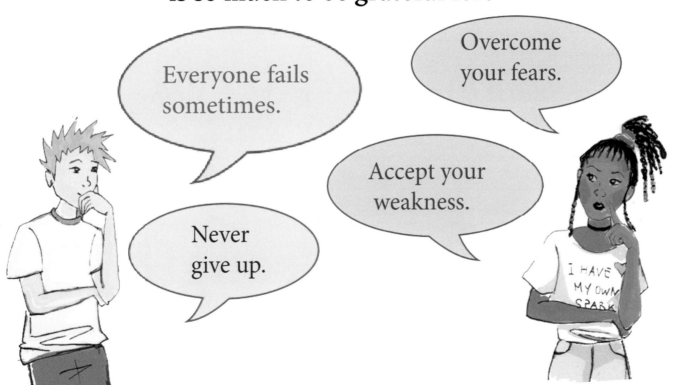

You can use these magical phrases to motivate yourself.

I will keep trying
I will accept my weaknesses
I am happy
I have strength

Gratitude Tree

Colouring words of affirmations

I FEEL SAFE
I AM SPECIAL
I WILL DO IT
I WILL LEARN
FROM MY
MISTAKES

Colouring Positive Pete and Mindful Molly

Famous Quotes

Success is not final, failure is not fatal: it is the courage to continue that counts. - Multiple Attributions

I have not failed. I have just found 10,000 ways that won't work. - Thomas A. Edison

My approach to cricket has been reasonably simple: It was about giving everything to the team, it was about playing with dignity and it was about upholding the spirit of the game. I hope I have done some of that. I have failed at times, but I have never stopped trying. It is why I leave with sadness but also with pride.
Rahul Dravid

Can you research about the influential figures on page 37? Pick one, draw their picture and write about their accomplishments and failure.

Journaling

Remember to write, draw or talk about your day. Write about your emotions, understand what makes you feel a certain way and how your negative feelings can be turned into positive ones. If you are angry or sad, what can you do to make yourself feel better? What makes you happy?

_____

_____

_____

_____

_____

Quotes by Positive Pete and Mindful Molly

Patience

What you want may not happen straight away. If you feel angry, breathe in deeply and let your anger float away. Do not act upon this emotion. Count backwards from 5 and allow yourself the time to rest your negative emotion.

Fear

Don't let your fear prevent you from achieving your goal. If you are scared of smiling at someone because they may not smile back, smile anyway.

Intention

Be true to yourself. Be kind. Ask yourself why you have made the choice.

Words of affirmation

Speak to others using words that will make them feel better. "You must believe in yourself."

Journaling

Write. Write. Write. It helps you think and understand yourself better. The answers are in your mind. You just need to search within yourself.

Visualisation

Make time for yourself. Remain quiet and let your mind paint a picture of something you want. Something that makes you feel great!

Meditation

Pick a quiet place. Take deep breaths. Prepare yourself to visualise.

Living in the Present

Don't keep worrying about what might happen or what happened in the past. Be present and appreciate what you have now.

Mindfulness
Go for a walk. Smell the fresh air. Taste an apple from your tree.

Gratitude
If you have woken up in the morning with negative energy hovering around you, stop and bring yourself back to the present. There is so much to be thankful for.

Glossary (The words are defined according to how they are used in the sentence in this book.)

Persevere: keep trying even if you fail
Consistent: repeating an action in order to master it
Anxiety: when you become distressed or uneasy
Meditation: clearing the mind, using deep breathing
Visualise: create a picture in your mind
Passionate: powerful feeling of love towards something you feel strongly about.